To:

From:

THE SISTER BOOK

TODD PARR

Megan Tingley Books
LITTLE, BROWN AND COMPANY
NEW YORK BOSTON

To Tammy, Morgan, Amelia, and Emma

Also by Todd Parr

  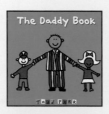   

A complete list of Todd's books and more information can be found at toddparr.com.

About This Book

The art for this book was created on a drawing tablet using an iMac, starting with bold black lines and dropping in color with Adobe Photoshop. This book was edited by Megan Tingley and Allison Moore and designed by Nicole Brown. The production was supervised by Erika Schwartz, and the production editor was Marisa Finkelstein. The text was set in Todd Parr's signature font.

There are all kinds of sisters.

Some sisters are big.

Some sisters are little.

Some sisters have long hair.

Some sisters have no hair.

Some sisters want to be scientists.

Some sisters want to be mermaids.

Some sisters help in the kitchen.

Some sisters help in the garage.

Some sisters like to hang out with you.

Some sisters like to spend time alone.

Some sisters yell when they're upset.

Some sisters cry.

Some sisters like to be dressy.

Some sisters like to be messy.

Some sisters look like you.

Some sisters look like themselves.

Some sisters live with you.

Some sisters live far away.

All sisters are a special part

of your family!

Sisters are very special. Sometimes they hug you, and sometimes they ♥ bug you. Be sure to tell them how much you love them. ♡ The End. XOXO Love, Todd